BiRDS OF A FEATHER

WRITTEN BY
Sita Singh

ILLUSTRATED BY
Stephanie Fizer Coleman

PHILOMEL BOOKS

PHILOMEL BOOKS

An imprint of Penguin Random House LLC, New York

First published in the United States of America by Philomel,
an imprint of Penguin Random House LLC, 2021.

Text copyright © 2021 by Sita Singh.
Illustrations copyright © 2021 by Stephanie Fizer Coleman.

Philomel Books is a registered trademark of Penguin Random House LLC.

Visit us online at penguinrandomhouse.com.

Library of Congress Cataloging-in-Publication Data is available.

Manufactured in China

ISBN 9780593116449

10 9 8 7 6 5 4 3 2 1

Edited by Liza Kaplan.
Design by Monique Sterling.
Text set in Carniola.

Artwork created digitally in Adobe Photoshop with
traditionally painted gouache and watercolor textures.

To my parents, Kokila & Navnit, for their
blessings and encouragement —S.S.

For Seth, always —S.F.C.

One spring morning, the Himalayan jungle welcomed a new generation of peachicks, including one named Mo.

Each one was covered in a coat of yellow or brown feathers.

Mo and his friends roosted high and low, caught ticks and termites, and screeched loud into the night.

Mo loved to roost, hunt, and screech. But what he loved most of all was playing hide-and-seek.

By the second summer, each peachick donned a crest.
They grew flight feathers. Tail feathers.

FLUFF FLUFF FLUFF!

Some had short tails. Some had long.

All the long-tailed peachicks turned into peacocks with
bright, bold, beautiful colors.

All except Mo. Mo looked different.

From the top of his crest to the tip of his tail, his feathers
shone white.

Mo didn't mind. The peacocks still did everything together.

But as time went on . . .
hide-and-seek wasn't quite as fun as it used to be.

Mo couldn't hide like the others.

He didn't have bright, bold, beautiful feathers.

Mo looked different. And he began to feel different, too.

But his friends did what friends do—

Mo shook off his worries.

He was glad to belong to such a great group of peacocks.

Soon, the jungle announced
its biggest day—

THE ANNUAL DANCE in THE RAIN

The young peacocks couldn't
wait to show off.
First rain! First dance!

They flocked to the Color Salon.
They flew to the Bird Boutique.

COLOR SALON

BRIGHTEN YOUR BLUES

RICHEN YOUR REDS

All the peacocks pranced. They admired themselves.

All except Mo.

Even with a fluff and a trim, Mo's feathers were no match for the others.

Mo looked different. Mo felt different. And now he also felt alone.

But his friends did what friends do—

You're still a peacock!

Colors don't make the bird!

You can do this!

Let's learn the dance!

"Neck tight! Feathers loose!
Spread your tail!"

S-T-R-E-T-C-H! S-T-R-E-T-C-H! S-T-R-E-T-C-H!

Feathers swung open.

The peacocks strutted. They swayed. Colors swirled all around.

Mo's friends shouted, *GO, MO, GO!*

But all he heard was, *NO, MO, NO!*

However hard Mo tried, he only saw what he didn't have—bright, bold, beautiful feathers.

Mo looked different. Mo felt different. He felt alone. And now he was sad, too.

On the big night, everyone gathered to welcome the first rain.
Everyone except Mo. Mo watched from a place in the trees.

Soon, black clouds took over the sky and raindrops hit the ground.
The peacocks were ready for their dance, but there was just one problem—

It was too dark to see.

The peacocks bumped into one another.
They stepped on one another's trains.

Their feathers rumpled and ruffled.
Everyone was in a fowl mood.

Then thunder crashed and lightning flashed.

Suddenly, Mo noticed a bright and brilliant glow.
He straightened his slouch and loosened his wings.

He looked all around until he realized—
the glow was coming from him!

Right away, Mo took flight.
In a swoop, he lit up the ground.

Yes, Mo was different. But now Mo saw what he'd had all along—
bright, bold, beautiful feathers. And his crest felt like a crown.

As lightning flashed, the hip-hoppers croaked, "He glows like the snow!"

The belly dancers trumpeted, "He's as bright as a lotus!"

The rock & rollers roared, "But we still can't see!"

Mo knew just what to do.

He stood tall. He strutted and swayed.

Then he fluttered his feathers and swung them open.

As Mo danced, light flickered! It flashed! The jungle glowed bright.
At last everyone could see!

The peacocks fanned their feathers and danced together.
Sounds of celebration echoed throughout the jungle.

Mo smiled. He flaunted his plume as wide as he could.
On and on, he danced. On and on, Mo called to the sky.

T·E·H·U·N·K

T·E·H·U·N·K

T·E·H·
U·N·K

That night, the rains didn't stop.
Neither did Mo.

And when his friends shouted again,
he heard them loud and clear.

Author's Note

I was born and raised in India. I have watched peacocks in farmlands all through my childhood, sometimes perched on the rooftops, sometimes prancing in the backyards, and at times dancing in the rains. I have also heard their loud screeches and collected their beautiful feathers. White peacocks are much rarer and I have always wondered about their unique and alluring beauty. The story of Mo is inspired by happy memories of watching peacocks as a child. I am proud to share this tale that introduces readers to a national symbol of the country of my birth.

Fun Facts About Peacocks

Did you know that the general name for the species we refer to as peacocks is actually "peafowl"? A peafowl family is made up of a peacock (the male), a peahen (the female), and numerous little peachicks (the babies). There are three types of peafowl in the world—Indian, green, and Congo—though Indian peafowl are the most common.

In peafowl, it is the male who has majestic tail feathers. These tail feathers make up 60 percent of a peacock's entire body length. They are mostly used to show off and attract a peahen.

Sometimes, when the cells of a peacock don't produce enough melanin and other types of pigmentation responsible for color, then a peacock is white. His condition is called leucism. But a leucistic peacock is different from an albino peacock, who has an absence of melanin.

Peacocks live mostly on farmlands and forests in warm regions. Since they live on land, they mainly feed on fruits, flowers, and seeds. But their favorite foods are ants, ticks, and termites.

Did you know that a group of peacocks is called a "party"? If you ever go near a party of peacocks, be careful. As much as these birds are social and like people, they can get aggressive and peck and scratch. They mostly do this as an act of self-defense.

When a peacock calls, it sounds like a scream or a screech. It is high-pitched and loud, especially during the monsoon season. In India, people believe that peacocks can predict the rain, and they call out and dance to welcome the monsoon season.

The Hindus also consider peacock feathers to bring good luck and prosperity. While one of the Hindu gods, Lord Krishna, is believed to wear a peacock feather in his crown, another one, Lord Kartikeya, is believed to ride on a peacock. Similarly, many other cultures around the world give great importance to peacocks and their feathers.